Let fear disapp...

is here!

Welcome to Trashland, a rubbish dump
at the edge of the world. It's home
to masses of mini-monsters in
real need of superheroes.

Luckily, whenever danger looms
large, Plog, Zill, Furp and Danjo
– the sensational Slime Squad –
are there to save the day!

Collect all the cool cards and check out
the special website for more slimy stuff:

www.slimesquad.co.uk

Don't miss the rest of the series:

THE SLIME SQUAD VS THE FEARSOME FISTS

And coming soon:

THE SLIME SQUAD VS THE CYBER-POOS

THE SLIME SQUAD VS THE SUPERNATURAL SQUIDS

Also available, these fantastic series:

COWS IN ACTION

ASTROSAURS

ASTROSAURS ACADEMY

www.stevecolebooks.co.uk

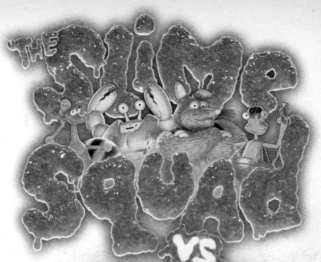

THE TOXIC TEETH

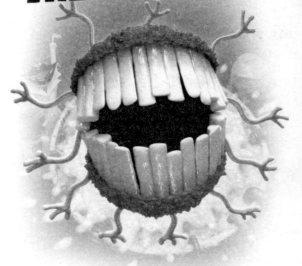

by Steve Cole

Illustrated by Woody Fox

RED FOX

THE SLIME SQUAD vs THE TOXIC TEETH
A RED FOX BOOK 978 1 862 30887 0

First published in Great Britain by Red Fox,
an imprint of Random House Children's Books
A Random House Group Company

This edition published 2010

1 3 5 7 9 10 8 6 4 2

The Random House Group Limited supports the Forest Stewardship
Council (FSC), the leading international forest certification
organization. All our titles that are printed on Greenpeace-approved
FSC-certified paper carry the FSC logo. Our paper procurement policy
can be found at www.rbooks.co.uk/environment.

Mixed Sources
Product group from well-managed
forests and other controlled sources
www.fsc.org Cert no. TT-COC-2139
© 1996 Forest Stewardship Council
FSC

Set in16/20pt Bembo Schoolbook by
Falcon Oast Graphic Art Ltd

Red Fox Books are published by Random House Children's Books,
61–63 Uxbridge Road, London W5 5SA

www.kidsatrandomhouse.co.uk
www.rbooks.co.uk

Addresses for companies within The Random House Group Limited can
be found at: www.randomhouse.co.uk/offices.htm

THE RANDOM HOUSE GROUP Limited Reg. No. 954009

A CIP catalogue record for this book is available from
the British Library.

Printed in the UK by CPI Bookmaque, Croydon

For Amy

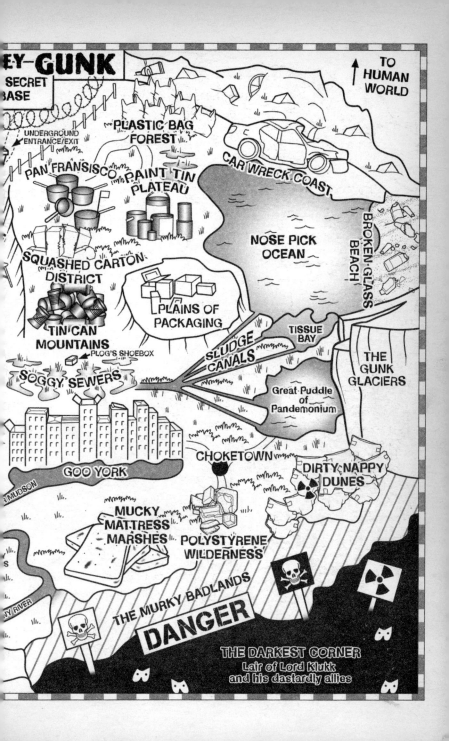

ONCE UPON A SLIME...

The old rubbish dump was far from anywhere. An enormous, mucky, rusty landscape of thousands of thrown-away things.

It had been closed for years. Abandoned. Forgotten.

And then Godfrey Gunk came along.

Godfrey wasn't just a mad scientist. He was a SUPER-BONKERS scientist! And he was very worried about the amount of pollution and rubbish in the world. His dream was to create marvellous mutant mini-monsters out of chemical goo – monsters who would clean up the planet by eating, drinking and generally devouring all types of trash.

So Godfrey bought the old rubbish dump as the perfect testing-ground and got to work.

Of course, he wanted to make good, friendly, peaceful monsters, so he was careful to keep the nastiest, most toxic chemicals separate from the rest. He worked for years and years . . .

And got nowhere.

In the end, penniless and miserable, Godfrey wrecked his lab, scattered his experiments all over the dump, and moved away, never to return.

But what Godfrey didn't know was that long ago, tons of radioactive sludge had been accidentally dumped here. And soon, its potent powers kick-started the monster chemistry the mad scientist had tried so hard to create!

Life began to form. Amazing mini-monsters sprang up with incredible speed.

Bold, inventive monsters, who made a wonderful, whiffy world for themselves from the rubbish around them – a world they named Trashland.

For many years, they lived and grew in peace. But then the radiation reached a lead-lined box in the darkest corner of the rubbish dump – the place where Godfrey had chucked the most toxic, dangerous gunk of all.

Slowly, very slowly, monsters began to grow here too.

Different monsters.

Evil monsters that now threaten the whole of Trashland.

Only one force for good stands against them. A small band of slightly sticky superheroes . . .

The Slime Squad!

Chapter One

SQUIDS, SQUADS AND SLIME-ADE

Behind a dark, dark rubbish dump called Trashland, there stood an even darker house. No one had lived there for years – no one human anyway.

But down in the cellar of the dark, dark house was a light, bright secret base for a bunch of marvellous mini-monsters with special slimy skills.

1

And right now, one of them was shouting – very, very loudly . . .

"Let fear disappear!" bellowed Plog the monster. "The Slime Squad is, er, close by?"

"No, no, no," groaned Zill, a black-and-white she-monster. "The Slime Squad is *here* – rhymes with *disappear*, remember?" She had the tail of a skunk, the legs of one and a half poodles and the patience of a saint – which Plog was testing to its limit. "Try again."

Plog nodded quickly. "Let fear disappear – the Slimy Squid is here!"

"Slimy *Squid*?" spluttered Zill. "What are you on about? If you're going to be our leader, you've got to be able to shout the team battle cry."

"I'm sorry," said Plog. "I still can't believe I'm actually *in* the Slime Squad, let alone yelling about it."

Zill's face softened. "*I* can," she said kindly.

Just a few short days ago, Plog had been a miserable monster living all alone in a sewer pipe. The closest he'd ever got to excitement had been watching his ever-helpful heroes, the Slime Squad, go into action on his smellyvision set.

3

Then, suddenly, the three members of that very Squad – Zill, Furp and Danjo – had called on him to help in the struggle against a new evil looming over their peaceful rubbish-dump world – the evil of mad, bad monsters grown from totally toxic waste, with awful ambitions to take control of Trashland . . .

Plog had helped the Squad to victory with a combination of natural bravery and *un*naturally yucky feet. Zill and the others had asked him to stay on as their leader, and he'd been overjoyed to accept. But sometimes he still felt unsure of himself, and this was one of those times.

"One more go," Plog said, with fresh determination. "Let fear drink a beer, the Slime Squad are . . . *deer*?"

"NOOOO!" cried Zill, shaking her snout. "It's here, it's HERE!"

Suddenly, a pale yellow frog-like monster in metal pants bounced into the room and stuck to a wall with his slimy hands and feet. "What's here? What?" His high-tech crash helmet caught the light as he peered about. "Nothing terrible, I hope?"

"Only my memory, Furp," Plog sighed, plucking at his long wiry whiskers. "I can't do our battle cry!"

"My dear Plog, it's simplicity itself."

5

Furp hopped down to the ground. He was clever and inventive, and rather grand as small monsters went. "Let fear disappear, the Slime Squad are—"

"Raring to go!" boomed a large red crab-monster, his six pincers and three sturdy legs a blur as he raced inside. "Whatever's going down – Danjo's in town!"

"Excellent, Danjo," said Furp. "You can help me try out a new invention of mine." He delved about in his oversized underwear and pulled out a corked bottle full of green liquid. "It's a drink I've created called Slime-ade. Puts the fizz back into your fozzicles."

Plog wasn't sure what his fozzicles were but he was certainly thirsty. "I'll get some glasses from the kitchen."

"No need, Fur-boy." Using her special slimy powers, Zill spat out a sticky strand of slime across to the grubby little kitchen at the back of the room. Like a sticky lasso, the slime-line looped around some glasses on the draining board – and with a jerk of her head, Zill yanked them back through the air.

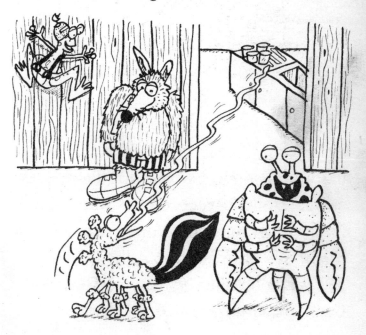

"To me!" Danjo neatly caught the glasses in his small pincers. His larger claws had the power to squirt hot and cold slime, so with the one on his right he filled each glass with slimy ice cubes.

Furp poured the Slime-ade and beamed. "Drink up, everyone!"

Zill took a sip – and spat it straight out again. "Yuck! That tastes like wet feet and soggy sugar!"

"And so it should," said Furp defensively. "Slime-ade is made by mixing fizzy pond water, a million half-chewed boiled sweets and a little of Plog's foot slime."

"Revolting," groaned Zill.

"I'll say," Danjo agreed. "All that sugar is bad for your teeth!"

Plog looked down at his tootsies and blushed. He wore heavy metal boots, full of water, at all times. He had to; if his feet ever dried out, they produced the nastiest, smelliest goo in the whole world. But crazy chemist Furp loved the stuff because he could put it to all kinds of loopy slime-tastic uses.

"Sorry, Furp," said Plog, setting down his glass. "But like my feet – Slime-ade stinks!"

"But . . . I've mixed up tons of the stuff!" Furp drained his glass and gave a crestfallen burp. "I can't drink it all by myself."

"Cheer up," said Danjo. "If any big horrible baddies show up with an evil plan, make them drink a bottle – that'll sort them out!"

"I almost wish some baddies *would* come along," said Zill, nudging Plog in his hairy ribs. "Fighting them would be more fun than training Fur-boy here."

Suddenly, a loud alarm went off in the room next door – *A-WOWW-WOWW-WOWW!*

Furp gasped as the radar dish on his helmet started twizzling around. "It's the 'Evil monster alert'," he declared. "From the All-Seeing PIE!"

Zill groaned. "I should watch what I wish for!"

"Come on, everyone," said Plog. He felt a tingle of excitement as he led the sprint towards the huge, human-sized door that led into the gigantic office beyond.

PIE – short for Perfect Intelligent Electronics – was the Slime Squad's mega-mechanical boss. Built, broken and abandoned by the same human scientist who'd unknowingly brought Trashland to life, PIE used his circuits and sensors to watch over the rubbish dump and the millions of mini-monsters who lived there. If any one of them was in trouble, he sent the Slime Squad off to help. That was how Plog had got involved with all this craziness in the first place . . .

"Ah, there you are," boomed a deep electronic voice from the super-computer that sat in the middle of the messy office.

Cables and components leaked from his smashed-in casing like electronic guts, but his monitor screen still glowed a garish green, and two dots and a curly bracket flickered there like a face as the Slime Squad assembled before him. "What kept you? My alarm went off five-point-seven seconds ago!"

"Sorry, PIE," said Plog.

"Furp's yucky Slime-ade must have clogged up our legs," Zill added.

"Then you should unclog them again quickly," PIE rumbled. "My sensors tell me that strange monsters are burgling the Dentists-R-Us building in Spare Part Canyon." His screen filled up with exclamation marks. "It's Trashland's largest dental centre."

"That's a funny place to rob," said Zill.

Plog nodded. There were lots of dentists in Trashland – since the monster population fed mostly on concrete, metal and chemical gloop, there had to be. But as Zill said, who would want to rob a dental centre?

"Maybe the robbers have a toothache," Furp suggested.

Danjo raised his pincers. "That'll be the least of their troubles when *we* catch up with them!"

"Right," Plog agreed. "Let fear disappear, the Slime Squad are, um, all clear . . ." He caught sight of Zill's despairing face. "All clear for *action*, I mean!"

"Nice recovery, Fur-boy," Zill said, a sparkle in her eyes. "Now, let's get to the Slime-mobile — we've got burglars to catch!"

Chapter Two
ALARM IN THE ALLEY

With his friends close behind, Plog raced
through a door in the skirting board. It
led to the Slime Squad's garage, where
the gang's super-charged, ultra-tough
turbo-truck was kept.

The Slime-mobile wasn't much to look at from the outside – because Furp had covered it in invisible paint! But today, something stood out – an enormous iron cauldron had been tied onto the Slime-mobile's roof rack . . .

Danjo skidded to a surprised stop. "What's that thing doing there – to help us see where we've parked?"

"Er . . . it's actually full of Slime-ade," said Furp sadly. "I thought you'd all love it so much I'd need to take a special supply wherever we went."

Zill shook her head as she climbed aboard. "The whole point of invisible transport is to make sure no one sees us coming or going!"

"I was planning to paint it invisible later," Furp protested.

"Well, there's no time to do anything about it now," said Plog, bundling Furp and Danjo into the Slime-mobile. "We must get to Spare Part Canyon and stop that robbery."

"Don't forget your costumes!" Zill cried, grabbing a golden leotard from the driver's seat. She wriggled into it and then jumped behind the huge steering wheel.

Danjo put on some golden shorts, while Plog pulled an identical pair over his head and tugged his long ears through the leg-holes.

17

Both of them took seats just behind Zill, while Furp hopped into his lav-lab at the rear – a space crammed with tables creaking under the weight of countless chemistry experiments, and a special slimy toilet the frog-monster used as a mixing bowl. Since Zill got very cross if the four of them didn't match when out on a mission, he swapped his pants and headgear for identical golden versions.

"Away we go, boys!" Zill started the engine, flicked on the headlights – and roared off at super-colossal, double-scary speed!

"Whoaaaaaaa!" yelled Plog, Danjo and Furp as the Slime-mobile zoomed away through a secret tunnel and out into Trashland. Soon they were tearing through the rubbishy landscape on their

way to Spare Part Canyon. Luckily, night had fallen so there weren't too many monsters about to notice the giant cooking pot on their invisible roof rack that seemed to be flying through the air.

Plog's tummy bubbled with nerves as he stared out of the windscreen. But in a matter of minutes they had reached the outskirts of Spare Part Canyon – a rugged district of factories and office blocks made entirely from scraps of dirty plastic and battered, rusting metal. The Tin Can Mountains he used to call home were distant shadows in the moonlight, and the rusting hulks of the Car Wreck Coast could barely be seen at all.

Danjo peered at a screen on the wall. "According to the map, this road should lead us straight there," he told Zill. "Dentists-R-Us is the widest building on the main street."

"That must be it up ahead!" Zill cried, as the Slime-mobile rocked and crunched over sheets of transparent packaging towards a massive block of metal and plastic dominating the neighbourhood.

"There's someone outside," Plog realized. "Three figures . . ."

Furp hopped forward to see. "They must be PIE's burglars!"

Two shadowy shapes were rolling big barrels out of an alleyway beside the building, while a third character, slimmer and taller than the others, watched from beside a white pick-up truck. As the Slime-mobile roared closer, the figures froze – and the tallest one pointed.

Zill groaned and Furp blushed. "Thanks to that big tub of Slime-ade on the roof, they can see us coming!"

Plog jumped up from his seat as the figures disappeared back up the alley. "Look, they're running away."

"Wherever they go, I'll follow them," Zill vowed, gripping the wheel as she swung the Slime-mobile off the path of packaging, screeched past the pick-up truck and bumped to a halt, parking across the entrance to the rusty alleyway.

21

Danjo jumped up. "Let's get to work, guys. When danger looms large, the Slime Squad cry—"

"Nobody move!" Plog bellowed, leaping out through the Slime-mobile's side doors and racing into the thick darkness of the alley.

"Actually we cry 'charge'." Danjo followed Plog out, his pincers raised and ready. "But you were close."

Furp hopped down to join them. "I thought we were right on top of those burgling baddies. Where did they go?"

Zill stuck her snout out through the doors and sniffed. "They . . ." She gasped. "Guys – I think they ran around the block. They're behind us!"

A slurping, whooshing sound started up suddenly – and with a squealing screech of rubber on rust, the entire Slime-mobile was dragged backwards by some mysterious force! Zill overbalanced and fell to the ground – only to find herself sliding after the Slime-mobile as though some giant vacuum cleaner was sucking her up . . .

"Zill!" Plog shouted. "Spit out a slime-line!"

With a flick of her jaws, Zill did exactly that. Plog caught the sticky strand with both hands – but then a fierce gale tore through the alley and blew the four friends off their feet!

Caught by surprise, they were sent tumbling like loose litter until the wind died down as quickly as it had started up, leaving them in a heap.

"First we were sucked in, the next we were blown away," Danjo groaned, flat on his back. "What happened?"

"That's an easy one, handsome," drawled a soft, breathy voice. "*We* happened."

Plog looked up in a daze and blinked as two large, round, podgy monsters rolled out from the alley's shadows to stand in a shaft of moonlight. One was red and the other was blue, but they each had short arms and legs, tiny black eyes and a mega-massive mouth that seemed as big as their whole body.

Then, a tall, slim, feminine figure followed them into sight. She had long legs, slender arms and wore a spotless white raincoat. But Plog gasped as he realised that the lady had something quite unexpected where her head should've been.

In place of a face she had an enormous pair of ruby red lips, with little green eyes shining just on top!

"We shifted your wheels 'cause they were blocking our getaway truck," said the lady with the lips. "They had to be removed. And the same goes for anyone or anything that gets in the way of Countess Kiss and the Gruesome Gobs!"

Chapter Three
GOBS DOING JOBS

As the Slime Squad got incredulously to their feet, Zill was first to find her voice. "Countess Who and the *Whats*?" she spluttered.

"Countess Kiss." The slender figure winked. "Don't my luscious lips just make you flip?" She smiled down at the blobs. "And these are my little Gruesome Gobs, Sukka and Blowdart."

"Stay back and don't try any tricks," wheezed Blowdart, the blue blobby ball. "Or I'll blow you away."

"And *I'll* suck you back up," sneered Sukka, the red one. "Then I'll spit you out like soggy cornflakes – and suck you back up AGAIN! And then I'll—"

"Yeah, thanks, I think we've got the threat now." Plog glared at Countess Kiss. "What are you up to? What's in those barrels you're stealing?"

"The finest floss, mouthwash and toothpaste you can get," said Blowdart. "We're stealing tons of the stuff."

"We need it for a top-secret evil experiment," Sukka explained.

"Enough, boys," snapped Countess Kiss. "Anyone ever tell you two you've got big mouths?"

"Er, yeah," said Sukka. "Everyone."

"I don't know what experiment you're on about, and I don't think I want to," said Plog. "But you'd better put those stolen things back right now."

Blowdart's tiny eyes narrowed. "No."

"Then we'll have to make you," growled Danjo.

"How dull," sighed Countess Kiss. "Excuse me while I put on some lip gloss . . ."

As she took a step back, her Gruesome Gobs pushed forwards with fierce expressions.

But Danjo was not to be put off. "If it's mouthwash you want," he snarled, "try rinsing with hot slime!" Flashing out his left pincer, he squirted red goo at Blowdart's blubbery blue body. But the Gruesome Gob simply blew with his gale-force breath and the slime was slung over Danjo and Plog! They reeled back, blinded and choking.

Zill scowled at Blowdart and Sukka. "Creeps like you should be kept on a lead!" With a snap of her snout she sent a slime-line shooting towards the Gruesome Gobs. But Sukka sucked it greedily into his mouth like a strand of slimy spaghetti and tugged it right out of Zill's open jaws! He gulped it down and stuck out his tongue, while a single, giant puff from Blowdart sent the she-monster crashing helplessly into Danjo. The two Squaddies collapsed in a black, white and crimson pile.

"I can see I shall have to bounce some sense into you!" cried Furp. He jumped from one wall of the alley to the other, and then back again, criss-crossing at dazzling speed before finally launching himself at the big-mouthed baddies. WHUMP! He smashed his crash helmet into Sukka and – CLANG! – his metal pants brained Blowdart. The Gruesome Gobs fell over in a daze as Furp sprung clear.

"Nice work, Furp," said Plog, wiping the last of the hot slime from his eyes. "You've given me a clear run at their boss lady."

"Is that a fact?" Countess Kiss pursed her slobbery, slug-like lips. "Come and get me, then, you sweet little bear-rat."

"Ugh!" Plog pulled a face as he charged towards her. "Making me sick won't save you."

"Then, perhaps *this* will!" To his surprise, instead of trying to run, the countess rushed towards him – and planted a cold, wet, lipsticky kiss on the end of his snout!

"Urrrgh . . . mmmmph," Plog spluttered. The countess had the worst breath he had ever smelled – a mix of pickled eggs, dirty toilets and rotting seagull bottoms. Desperately he tried to pull away, but she had latched on as though she meant to snog his snout off and refused to let go.

Plog grew dizzy as the awful smell and taste began to overcome him . . .

But then a wave of cold fizzy liquid broke over his furry face, shocking his senses awake like smelling salts. The countess broke off from her deadly kiss-attack, spitting and spluttering, and Plog collapsed to the ground.

Furp, Zill and Danjo were beside him in a second, their faces concerned. Plog groaned. "What happened?"

Zill held up an empty bottle. "We gave you a splash of Slime-ade!"

"Lucky I made so much after all," Furp beamed.

"Yuck!" Countess Kiss leaned on her Gruesome Gobs. "That's the most revoltingly sweet concoction I've ever tasted. Come on, boys, we've wasted enough time here. And I do believe that the froggy one's bouncing about has rather weakened this alleyway . . . Don't you think so, Sukka?"

With a nasty chuckle, Sukka turned to the towering wall beside them and sucked in a sharp breath. The heavy plastic and metal began to wobble and shake.

"Uh-oh," said Zill as big black cracks appeared in the brickwork. "Plog, get up, quickly!"

"I'm afraid our smooch has left your leader in a daze," crowed Countess Kiss. "And now it's time to kiss you *all* goodbye!" She swept away into the darkness with her Gobs at her heels.

"The whole wall's caving in!" shouted Furp. "We've got to get away."

"But we can't leave Plog," Zill wailed.

"Look out!" cried Danjo.

But it was too late. The teetering wall smashed down on the Slime Squad with colossal, crushing force.

As the awful echoes of destruction faded, a pick-up truck roared away from the scene of the crime – and the evil laughter of Countess Kiss and the Gruesome Gobs rose mockingly into the night . . .

Chapter Four
COMPLETELY DENTAL

For a minute nothing stirred in the alley. Then, slowly, smoke swirled up from the pile of plastic and metal debris as it started to melt. Finally, Danjo burst out from beneath the remains of the wall, the molten mess sizzling on his tough, crimson skin. "Free!" he gasped.

Plog got up wearily behind him.

"Good work, Danjo. If you hadn't whizzed up that slime-ice barrier to protect us from the wall-fall, we'd have been squashed flat."

Teeth chattering, Furp poked his head up, his crash helmet scuffed and dented. "And if you hadn't then used your hot slime to melt a way back out, we'd have f-f-f-frozen to death!"

Zill got busy with all six legs and kicked a path through the remaining debris. "Countess Slobber-chops and her miserable munchkins will be long gone by now." She scowled. "But we'll get them. Won't we, Plog?"

Plog realized that Zill, Danjo and Furp were all looking at him. He gulped. "Er, of course we'll get them. They just took us by surprise, that's all."

Furp nodded sadly. "The workers at Dentists-R-Us will certainly get a surprise when they turn up tomorrow and find all their toothpaste, floss and mouthwash gone."

"Why would Lip-lady and the Gobs want to steal dentist stuff?" Danjo wondered. "They didn't seem to have any teeth."

"Did you smell the countess's breath?" Plog shuddered. "She needs some mouthwash all right!"

"But that breath of hers is clearly a powerful weapon," said Furp. "Why should she want to get rid of it?"

Zill shrugged. "Perhaps she has a date tonight."

"She'll have a date with us soon enough," Danjo growled menacingly. "And *she'll* be the one who pays."

Just then, Furp's radar dish started to spin. "I'm picking up a message from PIE," he realized.

"That didn't go very well, did it?" PIE's electronic voice crackled out from Furp's helmet. "They got away!"

"Did you see where they went?" Plog asked eagerly.

"No," said

PIE. "My local sensors were blinded by the dust from that collapsing wall. But something has come to my attention here at the base. Return at once!"

Soon, the Squad were zooming back to their secret base. All the way back, Plog couldn't stop thinking about the horrible countess and her mouthy mates. *Why did they burgle a big dentist's?* he thought for the fiftieth time. *With powers like theirs they could help themselves to anything . . .*

"Nearly there," Zill announced, steering the speeding Slime-mobile towards the cliff-like wall of a rusty, yellow skip. At the last moment, a hidden door in the side slid open to let them through. Stamping on the brake pedal with three of her feet, Zill brought the Slime-mobile skidding to a stop in the Squad's underground garage. "Now, why don't you boys take that silly cauldron of Slime-ade down from the roof while I see just how cross PIE is."

"Fair enough," said Furp.

Zill jumped from the Slime-mobile and trotted away down the dark

passage towards the chink of light at the
far end. Furp climbed up the side of
the Slime-mobile to the
super-sized cauldron
while Danjo crawled
underneath it to
cut through the
ropes.
Stiff and sore
from his battering,
Plog stood for a
moment with a feeling of relief. He
loved the secret base – it was much nicer
than the soggy shoebox-in-a-sewer that
had been his last home, and so much
safer . . .

Suddenly, Zill's voice echoed down
the tunnel. "Plog!" she yelled. "RAT!"

Plog frowned. "What have I done
now?"

"Not you," she squealed. "HERE!"

Furp quickly grabbed a torch from his
pants and shone it into the gloom.

Danjo stuck his head out from under the Slime-mobile – and like Furp and Plog, he gasped in horror at the sight of a huge, horrifyingly hairy sewer rat pushing through the door at the end of the passage!

With a menacing squeal, it loomed over Zill . . .

"Hang on!" Plog sprinted to the rescue. He knew he had to be fast. Sewer rats were deadly with their sharp, chisel-like teeth. CLANG! SPLOSH! went his feet in his big tin boots as he approached. CLONG! SPLISH!

Distracted by the noise, the rat turned to stare at Plog. Zill quickly spat out a slime-line and twirled it round the rat's front paws, tying them together. It turned, lashed out with its tail and thwacked her, sending her tumbling into Plog's path. "OOF!" He tripped over her and crashed to the floor. The towering sewer rat reared up and opened its drooling jaws . . .

Just as Danjo shot a ball of slime-ice into its open mouth! "Bull's eye!" he cried, running up. "Or 'rat's mouth', anyway."

With a muffled squeak, the rat tried to spit out the big frozen slime-ball but couldn't – it was lodged too firmly between its cheeks. And as Plog stared up in amazement, he realized that the vile vermin had other problems too.

It had no teeth at all!

"STOP MUCKING ABOUT OUT THERE," came PIE's tetchy shout from the room beyond. "That rat can't do much to hurt you, as you can see. I only allowed it into the base to show you all its curious condition."

"Thanks, PIE," said Zill drily, getting back up. "I always wanted to see a rat with no teeth."

"A curious condition indeed," said Furp, hopping closer. "Its teeth haven't snapped off or broken, they've been . . . pulled out."

"Precisely," PIE confirmed. "Every one of this rat's sixteen teeth have been carefully removed. What's more, my sensors have found several other rats in the same condition."

The toothless rat finally spat out the ice-ball and untangled its paws. But luckily it was in no mood to mess with mini-monsters. Plog watched as it shuffled off along the tunnel with a fed-up squeak, heading for the exit.

Furp hopped through the door in the skirting board to rejoin the All-Seeing PIE. "Who would want to extract a rat's teeth?"

"Rats are not the only victims of this dotty animal dentist," said PIE gravely. His screen flickered, and then the image of a small, sweet animal sucking a seed appeared. "Here is a picture I took earlier of a field mouse with no front teeth in Broken Furniture Valley."

Zill sighed. "Poor thing!"

"Quite," agreed PIE. "And here is a toothless ant . . ."

A close-up of a red ant with even redder gums showed on the screen.

"Not to mention a fangless fox," PIE continued. "Lastly, I'd like to show you this picture of a worm and a flower."

Zill frowned. "But worms don't have teeth."

"I know," said PIE. "It's nothing to do with the tooth business, I just thought it was a nice picture."

But Plog could not be distracted. "Only a dentist would have the skill to take out so many different types of teeth," he murmured. "But why would they want to?"

Furp shook his head, baffled. "We know that Countess Kiss and the Gruesome Gobs are stealing dental tools – maybe they're forcing dentists to work for them?"

"I feel sure this is all part of some sinister plot," boomed PIE, "and those wicked monsters are in it up to their menacing mouths." In a flash, his screen changed to show a large, slightly grubby building in the shape of a giant tooth, rising up from the middle of a narrow rubbish-filled ditch. "Now, pay attention – this is Trashland's Mouth Museum, on the outskirts of

the Squashed Carton District."

Zill looked unimpressed. "A mouth museum? It sounds pants."

"Right," said Danjo. "Who would want to go there?"

"Very few monsters at all," PIE told them. "But while you were gone, I checked my security camera tapes for unusual activity. And last night, two large blobs with even larger gobs were in the area."

"Sukka and Blowdart," Furp realized. "Then . . . the Mouth Museum could well be Countess Kiss's next target!"

"We have to pay it a visit right away," said Plog. "We must get *tooth* the bottom of this mouthy mystery – and the sooner, the better!"

Chapter Five

THE MAD MUSEUM

While the Slime Squad were getting ready for action, Countess Kiss and her Gruesome Gobs were hard at work in a gloomy, but very minty-smelling, underground lair.

"More mouthwash!" the countess hollered.

"We've poured in sixty-four barrels already," Sukka protested.

"DO IT!"

she screeched. "And add more toothpaste while you're at it."

Sukka did as he was told, up-ending two more barrels into an enormous tank of white bubbling goo, while Blowdart stirred the mint-stinking mess with an enormous dental pick. "Try the Life Lever again, mistress," he hissed. "Maybe this time it will work."

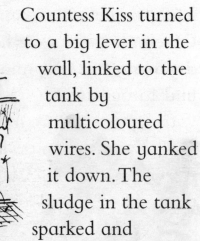

Countess Kiss turned to a big lever in the wall, linked to the tank by multicoloured wires. She yanked it down. The sludge in the tank sparked and bubbled with weird, antiseptic energy . . .

And then, with a very rude noise, the bubbling stopped and the tank was still.

"I am a demon dentist and I have

followed all the instructions," the countess whispered. "Why is there no spark of life?"

Sukka sighed. "The master will not be pleased."

Countess Kiss nodded. "I had better call Lord Klukk." She crossed to a special smellyvision set close by and pressed the big red button on the top. The screen flashed and flickered and then a dark shape appeared – the shadow of a large, bird-like creature with a cruel beak and a sinister wobbly bit on top of its head.

"Well?" demanded the creature in a cold throaty squawk. "What is it, Countess Kiss?"

"I . . . I'm so sorry, oh great and evil genius," she stammered. "But Experiment T has failed yet again. We have followed all your instructions, but there are no signs of life."

"Then clearly we must add another, more toxic, substance to the mixture." Lord Klukk considered. "Did the Slime Squad try to stop your robbery tonight?"

"Yes," the countess confirmed. "But we beat them."

"They are bound to come looking for you. You must *buk-buk*-be ready." He clucked softly to himself. "Yes . . . I think I know the final ingredient that will *buk-buk*-bring Experiment T to life — and where you can find it!"

Zill drove the Slime-mobile to the Mouth Museum. It stood in private grounds, set back from the dented houses in the rest of the Squashed Carton District, an enormous tooth-shaped tower. The stars twinkled and the moon shone overhead, reflected in the milk-bottle tops that lay scattered about the museum's weed-gardens like silver lily-pads.

"Here we are." As Zill parked outside the building, she heard the giant cauldron of Slime-ade sloshing about on top of the roof and sighed. "I wish you could've taken that thing down. This is a classy neighbourhood."

"No time," said Plog, opening the doors. "Countess Kiss and her plug-ugly pals might strike anywhere at any time – and if they do, ordinary monsters could get hurt."

Danjo nodded, rubbing his back with two of his smaller pincers. "This *extra*-ordinary monster is still hurting from the last time we tangled!"

The four of them got out. The museum grounds were quiet and still as Plog led the way to a front door made of damp plywood. He knocked on it loudly. "Hello? Sorry it's late, but can we come in?"

"Visitors!" came a posh, muffled voice from inside.

56

"Finally, my museum has visitors . . ."
The door was thrown open and a
skinny buck-toothed
yellow monster in a
white coat stared
out. His four
arms – like the
long spikes on his
head – seemed all
aquiver as he bowed
down low. "Gracious
me . . . *four* visitors!
Four marvellous mouth-lovers!
Four inquisitive seekers of the tooth,
the whole tooth and nothing but the
tooth . . ."

Zill cleared her throat and pointed to
her golden leotard. "Um, actually, we're
the Slime Squad."

"You are?" The monster straightened
up in baffled delight. "You are! Celebrity
visitors! Zill, Furp, Danjo and . . . and
the one with pants on his head!"

"Plog," sighed Plog. "Who are you?"

"I am Mercurio Curio, Master Curator of the Mouth Museum," he said grandly. "Your guide to all things dreamily dental."

"Well, we're on the lookout for some bad monsters in the area," said Furp. "Have you seen anyone suspicious hanging about?"

"Like, a thin lady-monster with giant lips accompanied by two big-mouthed balls?" Danjo added.

"I haven't seen a soul," Curio declared. "But if I did spot anyone, I'd make them take the tour of my magnificent exhibits. Like this!" He grabbed each member of the Slime

Squad by the arm and hauled them through the front door. "Come! Let me start *filling* you in, ha, ha. First on our tour is an exact reconstruction of Trashland's very first dental surgery, which was run by a short-sighted monster called Yankett Screeming."

Curio pushed them into a room with nothing inside but a small wooden stool, several big hammers and red stains all over the walls.

Danjo frowned. "This Yankett guy was really a dentist?"

"Oh, yes," said Curio. "A mad, rubbish dentist, but a dentist nevertheless." He propelled his visitors out again and into a corridor.

"And look! Along here I keep all kinds of dentist's tools, from a simple toothpick to this mega-drill built to treat the giant teeth of the Purple Ponkwasher."

"What's a Purple Ponkwasher?" Furp inquired.

"No one knows." Curio gazed happily at the whopping great machine. "But if we ever discover one and its teeth are aching, this is just the thing to sort it out!"

Zill whispered in Plog's ear: "He's a loony!"

Plog nodded. "But with all this dentist's stuff lying about, he's *got* to be a target for the Gob Gang."

Danjo pointed a pincer towards a big metal door at the end of a side-corridor. "Er, Curio? What have you got through here?"

"Aha!" said Curio. "Behind that door I keep my priceless display of old teeth."

Plog pulled a face. "Pardon?"

"For years now," Mr Curio said proudly, "I've been travelling the land going through dentists' dustbins – rescuing all the dodgy teeth they've pulled out and bringing them back here to put on show. I've got thousands and thousands of them!"

"Gross!" said Zill. "No wonder no one ever comes here."

"How dare you, madam!" Curio glared at her, then ran to the door and unlocked it with a large key. "You'll eat those words when you've seen the sheer magnificence of fifty-three thousand broken, rotten teeth on display . . ." He pushed open the door. "Ta-daaaaa!"

Zill, Plog, Furp and Danjo all looked inside and gasped.

"Told you so!" said Curio smugly. But then *he* looked inside and gasped too.

Row upon row of clear glass display cases stood empty. There were no teeth in the room at all. But at the back, there lurked two very familiar blobs with grinning, gaping mouths . . .

Sukka and Blowdart – the Gruesome Gobs – were already inside the museum!

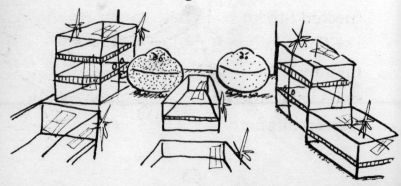

Chapter Six

GRABBED BY THE GOBS

"My old tooth collection!" yelled Curio. "My priceless pearly-whites, they've all been stolen!"

Plog frowned as he saw that neither Sukka nor Blowdart were carrying any bags or boxes. "All right," he growled. "What did you do with those teeth?"

"Wouldn't you like to know," sneered Sukka.

"They . . . they must have swallowed them!" Zill declared.

As if in agreement,
Blowdart stretched
his mouth wide
and burped so
loudly that it
rattled the glass in
the display cases – and
knocked Curio and the Slime Squad off
their feet! With nasty chuckles, the two
Gruesome Gobs charged past them and
out through the door.

Furp jumped up. "They're getting
away!"

"After them!" yelled Plog.

Zill and Danjo were about to follow
when Curio grabbed hold of them both.
"No! Don't leave me! They'll come
back and get me!" He threw back his
head and yelled. "Help! Murder! Tooth
robbery!"

"I'll stay with him," Zill told Danjo.
"Get after Plog and Furp and I'll join
you when I can."

But Danjo *couldn't* get away – the wailing Curio was clinging on to his golden shorts so tightly he almost pulled them down! "Let go!" the crab-monster protested. "Those

mouthy blobs are too tough for our friends to tackle alone." But Curio was too busy crying and wailing and carrying on to hear a thing.

Then Zill grabbed Danjo's arm too. "I just had a horrid thought – Countess Kiss!"

"That *is* a horrid thought," Danjo agreed. "If her Gruesome Gobs were here in this room – where has she got to?"

★

Plog and Furp chased after the Gruesome Gobs through corridors lined with dental equipment, sacks full of old fillings and even close-up photographs of famous fangs.

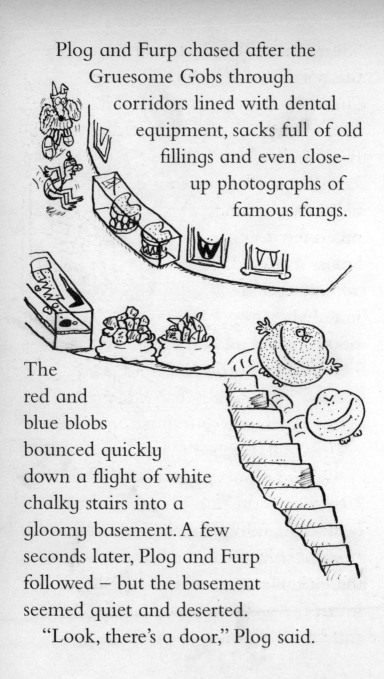

The red and blue blobs bounced quickly down a flight of white chalky stairs into a gloomy basement. A few seconds later, Plog and Furp followed – but the basement seemed quiet and deserted.

"Look, there's a door," Plog said.

"Sukka and Blowdart must have gone through here." Carefully, he crept up on the door – then kicked it open. Furp hopped inside and Plog went in warily after him. But aside from an old dentist's chair and a few tooth braces scattered about, the room was empty.

"Where did they go?" Furp wondered. Suddenly, the door slammed shut behind them. Plog whirled round but could already hear the key turning in the lock. He ran to the door, banged on it, but the only response was the sinister chuckle of a Gruesome Gob.

"There was nowhere to hide out there," shouted Plog in frustration. "How could we have missed them?"

But before Furp could answer, a sucking, squelching, whistling sound started up at the keyhole. "Oh, no – it must be Sukka!" he realized. "He's sucking all the air out of this room!"

Plog was already staggering. "It's getting harder to breathe," he gasped, pounding on the door with all his strength. Furp joined him, kicking and punching and even head-butting the metal with his crash helmet. But it was no good. The door wouldn't budge.

Plog's vision began to blur and soon the world was spinning around him. He sank to his knees.

"Well done, my gorgeously gruesome Gobs," came a familiar female purr from outside. "You've bagged the two slimy Squaddies we need . . ."

"Countess Kiss," Plog groaned.

"We're her prisoners," said Furp faintly. "But what does she want with us?"

Then the last breath of air was sucked through the keyhole and Plog and Furp fell unconscious to the floor . . .

Up above, in the main museum, Zill and Danjo were searching for their friends. Unable to leave Mr Curio on his own, they had been forced to take him along.

But since he was shivering, clinging
on to their legs and acting generally
terrified, it was slowing them down
a lot.

"Mr Curio," said Zill patiently, "we've
searched the upper floors and there's still
no sign of Furp and Plog. They must be
in the basement."

Curio groaned. "Please don't go down
there! It's gloomy! It's scary!"

"It's the only place we haven't
looked," said Danjo gruffly. "Come on,
let's go."

Carrying the reluctant Curio between them, Zill and Danjo staggered down the chalky steps. They searched all around the basement, but there was no one to be found and no sign of a struggle. The only side room contained an old dentist's chair and a few broken tooth braces – nothing more.

"They've gone," Zill breathed. "Plog, Furp, Sukka, Blowdart – somehow they've all vanished into thin air!"

Chapter Seven
VAT'S TERRIBLE!

Plog was woken by a terrible pong, like a million rotten fish exploding in a stink-bomb factory. His eyes snapped wide open – to find the loathsome lips of Countess Kiss hovering just above his face.

"Wake up, sleepy-head," she whispered. "You have something I need."

"Ugh!" Plog gasped. "Get away from me!" He tried to scramble up, but strong, fine cords cut into his fur. He realized he'd been tied up with dental floss and dumped on a dirty floor in a large, echoing chamber. The walls were lined with very big dental tools and strange control panels glowing spearmint-green. Cables ran from these uncanny instruments, connecting to a gigantic oval vat that filled the middle of the room. "I'm guessing this isn't part of the museum," Plog said slowly. "How did I get here?"

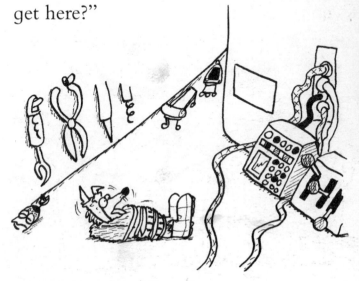

A smirking Blowdart bounced up beside his mistress. "You fell for our trap, sucker."

"Don't call him a sucker," said Sukka, peering out from behind the countess's legs. "It's rude to *proper* suckers, like me."

Plog ignored them both. "What is this place?" he demanded. "Where's Furp?"

"I'm right beside you, my dear Plog," said Furp gloomily. Plog craned his neck and saw the frog-monster was also flossed up, just behind him. "As for this place, well . . ."

Countess Kiss's giant lips twitched into a smile. "This is my Evil Experiments Lab, designed by my master – the mighty Lord Klukk."

"Klukk!" breathed Plog, who had come across the evil monster before. "The same Lord Klukk who sent evil fist-monsters into Trashland to steal money? Money he could use to fund his diabolical schemes to take over the world?"

"No," said Sukka. "A different one, who paints pretty pictures and is nice to his mum."

Furp frowned. "Really?"

"OF COURSE NOT!" the countess thundered, and Blowdart and Sukka laughed. "Lord Klukk needed the money to build labs like this one.

So when you and your Slime Squad friends spoiled his plans, he came to me for cash and assistance." She stuck her lips up in the air. "Dentistry has made me rich – that is how I can afford such talented servants as Sukka and Blowdart. But money alone is not enough. I want POWER."

"Along with a bit of lip gloss and a chapstick now and then," jeered Plog.

"Lord Klukk has promised he will give me a kingdom of my own if I help him conquer Trashland," hissed Countess Kiss. "And so I funded this evil lair and – with the aid of my Gruesome Gobs – gathered all the ingredients Lord Klukk required."

"Required for what reason, madam?" Furp demanded. "What's all this for?"

Countess Kiss threw open her arms. "To create NEW LIFE!" She snapped her fingers, and her Gruesome Gobs rolled away to a pair of control panels beside the oval vat. They hit some switches and blindingly bright lights shone down from above. The vat hummed with power. A window opened up in its side to reveal a thick white paste.

"Wow," said Plog. "You've created some white goop that sits in a jar. Congratulations."

Countess Kiss smiled. "You have not yet seen what lurks within. Behold . . . Experiment T!"

Sukka pressed a big blue button. With a menacing hum, something began to stir inside the vat. A platform pushed up from the thick depths. Something vast and jagged lay upon it, gleaming pearly white in the spotlights. Lots of long, spindly arms and legs emerged from the block of its body like lengths of toothpaste squeezed by a clumsy giant.

Plog and Furp both gasped in horror. It seemed that the thing had no eyes, no ears, no nose and no lips. But, boy, did it ever have a mouth.

In fact, it *was* a mouth.

A titanic set of terrifying teeth!

"Experiment T is our mouth-tastic marvel," hissed Countess Kiss. "His proper name is . . . *Toxitooth*!"

"Toxitooth, indeed." Furp looked flabbergasted. "However did you concoct such a thing?"

"The recipe is simple enough – if you are a genius." The countess smiled.

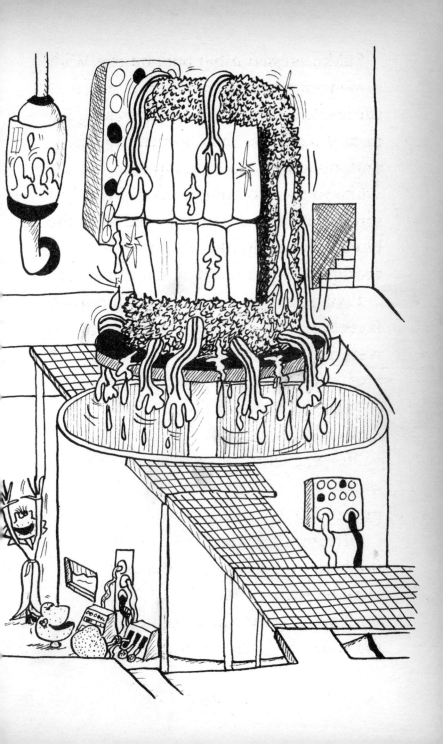

"First, take two tablespoons of ultra-toxic waste and a pinch of radiation. Mix with several tons of toothpaste and mouthwash. Add the fangs of wild animals to give cunning and savagery . . . Throw in a million manky monster teeth from the Mouth Museum to ensure plenty of bite . . . Cook for seventeen days at poison-gas-mark six and, hey presto – you are just one secret ingredient away from bringing your very own mouth-monster to life."
She smiled and jabbed a finger down at Plog. "A secret ingredient that YOU possess – that potent slime that dribbles from your horrible tootsies."

"What?" Beneath his orange fur, Plog felt himself turn pale. "No! My slime can't help you. You don't know what you're talking about!"

"Lord Klukk does." The countess smiled cruelly. "The

Slime Squad pose the only serious threat to his plans, so he has studied each of you very carefully. He knows that you, Plog, have the most powerful slime in Trashland – and that you, Furp, have the chemistry skills to know just how to use it. Together you will bring to life our mad mouth monster . . . and Toxitooth shall be unleashed onto the world!"

"Never!" cried Furp.

"If you don't," said the countess, "you and your friend will be squished, scrunched and squangled."

Furp
gulped.
"Er . . . well,
maybe not
quite never, then."

Plog looked at
him. "But we *can't* help
them, Furp! They're
evil!"

"We must, Plog." Suddenly,
Furp winked! Then he turned
back to the countess. "Now then,
I shall need to be untied and given
lots of equipment . . ."

Good old Furp must have a plan, Plog
realized, eyeing the silent Toxitooth with
a shiver. *Whatever it is – I just hope it
works!*

Meanwhile, growing more and more
worried about the whereabouts of their
friends, Zill and Danjo were searching
the grounds of the Mouth Museum.

Mr Curio seemed happy now to stay inside by himself, which was a big relief and meant they could hunt all the faster. But they could find no trace of Plog and Furp and not a single sign of the Gobs or their mistress.

"Let's get back to the Slime-mobile and ask PIE if he's spotted them," Zill suggested.

Danjo nodded and unlocked the doors. But as he did so, Zill frowned.

"Wait a second," she said. "Old Curio unlocked the door of the tooth vault to show us in – but Sukka and Blowdart were already inside. How did they get in through a locked door?"

"Good question," said Danjo slowly – and then he gasped. "Maybe they dug a tunnel and got in through a secret trap door or something?"

"That could explain how they spirited away all the teeth," Zill realized. "They might even have smuggled out Plog and Furp that way too! Come on, let's see." She galloped back to the front door and knocked hard. "Mr

Curio, it's us. We think the Gruesome Gobs have a secret way in and out of your museum. That must be how they got inside your vault when it was locked from the outside."

"We need to search every nook and cranny till we find it," Danjo added. "And every crook and nanny while we're at it!"

Curio's fearful face appeared at the door. "You . . . you'd better come in."

"Thanks." Danjo and Zill pushed inside and ran along the corridor to the tooth vault.

"Hold on," said Curio, pushing ahead of them. "I'll just unlock it for you." He turned a key and opened the heavy door – but the moment Zill and Danjo went through, he slammed it shut and locked them inside!

"Hey!" shouted Zill. "What's the big idea?"

Curio slid back an iron shutter to reveal a small grille over a window in the metal door.

"You were quite right," he called, pressing his face up against the protected glass. "The Gobs *do* have a secret way in and out of the museum. They've built a secret lab underneath the basement, and you get to it through a trap door."

"What?" Danjo frowned. "Then, Sukka and Blowdart didn't sneak inside this vault at all . . ."

"Correct," said Curio cheerfully. "I let them in. Forgive my little deception, but I've been working for Countess Kiss all along." He chuckled merrily. "I kept you out of the way while she got hold of your friends – and now I'm afraid you must stay locked up here until our plans are complete!"

Chapter Eight

TRICKS, TEETH AND TERROR

Zill stared helplessly at Danjo. "So that's why Curio grabbed us when we saw the Gruesome Gobs," she said. "So Sukka and Blowdart could catch Plog and Furp without having to fight us too!"

Danjo banged on the grille in the door and Curio took a worried step back. "You sneaky, bottom-headed poop-scooper!" the crab-creature cried. "Why would you help anyone as nasty as Countess Kiss and her mouthy mates?"

"Nasty? Nonsense. The countess is a sweet angel," said Curio. "*You're* the nasty ones. She told me how you picked on her and her friends . . ."

"Picked on her?" Zill shook her head. "That lippy old boot is tricking you. She tried to kill all four of us!"

"You must be mistaken," Curio insisted. "She's gentle and sweet and shares my love of teeth. She believes in my museum! And, with the help of your friends, the countess and her Gobs will soon complete their magnificent, megatastic tooth-creature."

Danjo gulped. "Their *what*?"

"A living set of gigantic jaws!" Curio said dreamily. "Imagine the pulling power of an exhibit like that. Monsters will come from all over Trashland to see such a thing, and my museum will finally be the mega-success it deserves to be." His voice hardened as he slid back the cover on the grille in the door. "So you'll just have to stay in here until they've finished. All right?"

"He's a total fruitcake," Zill groaned. "We've got to get out of here."

"But how?" Danjo muttered. "This vault is made of thick metal. It'll take ages for my hot slime to burn through it – and Furp and Plog must need our help right now!"

Down in the underground lab, Plog had been tied to a couch and his wet metal boots prised off to expose his ugly oversized feet.

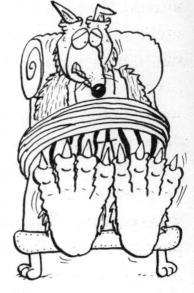

Furp stood beside him, studying a jar of white goo from the vat, waiting for Plog's tootsies to dry out so that the toxic slime would begin to pour. A bored-looking Sukka kept guard, while Blowdart peeled big, mouldy grapes for Countess Kiss at the back of the lab.

"Furp, this is awful," Plog moaned. "I can't believe that Klukk and Kiss are going to use us to bring their giant gnashers to life."

"If my plan works, we'll be doing just the opposite," Furp whispered, putting down the jar. "Your foot slime is extremely powerful, right? Just a few drops and a quick zap of electric power would be enough to bring Toxitooth to life." He lowered his voice still further.

"So what happens if we add a couple of *litres* of your foot slime, hmmm?"

Plog smiled slowly. "It would spoil the whole mixture?"

"Exactly!" Furp chuckled. "Poison the monster, overload the chemicals and probably blow the entire vat to  smithereens." His smile faded. "Of course, if it works, we will be doomed. Lord Klukk and the countess will kill us both. But at least Trashland will be safe."

"Maybe we can escape in the confusion," said Plog. "Or maybe Zill and Danjo will find us and rescue us! There's always a chance."

"That's enough talking," snarled Sukka.

"And far too much whiffing!" called Countess Kiss, her lips puckering at the glowing yellow slime oozing down from Plog's feet. "I can smell that stuff from here — and I haven't even got a nose!"

"It packs a pong strong enough to sock the conk off an alligator," Furp agreed, winking at Plog as he scraped

the gooey drops into a clean jar. "But don't knock this slime. It's going to bring your toothy terror to life . . . And I've just worked out how much we need."

"You have?"

Countess Kiss jumped up. "Then . . . we are ready for the final experiment?" She ran over and snatched the jar from Furp's froggy grip. "I must tell Lord Klukk. He will want to see this . . ."

As Furp quickly put Plog's tin boots back in place and filled them with water to stop the slime, Blowdart bounced over to the special two-way smellyvision in the corner of the EEL. Its screen started to flash black and red, and then Lord Klukk's sinister shadowy shape appeared. "Greetings," hissed the figure.

"So you're the wicked Lord Klukk, are you?" Furp enquired.

"Indeed I am, frog-monster," said Klukk. "And hello again to you, buk-buk-bear-rat thing. How fitting that the very same slime you once used to spoil my plans shall now allow me to triumph."

"Why are you hiding?" Plog demanded. "Why don't you show yourself?"

"When I appear to the people of Trashland, it will buk-buk-be as their leader." He chuckled and clucked with evil mirth. "And that glorious moment is drawing ever nearer – thanks to you."

"Why make a giant mouth-monster?" Furp wondered.

"I actually tried to buk-buk-buy a giant buk-buk-bum-monster," Lord Klukk confessed. "Sadly, it had to go buk-buk-back to the shop."

Plog frowned. "Why?"

"The buk-buk-bum had a crack in it!" Klukk guffawed at his rubbishy joke, and Countess Kiss and the Gruesome Gobs quickly joined in. "Now, frog-face – are you certain that you have correctly calculated the amount of foot slime to buk-buk-bring Toxitooth to life? Remember – you and your friend shall DIE if you are wrong."

Furp glanced gravely at Plog. "I know what I am doing."

"Good." Klukk hissed with pleasure. "Then, Countess Kiss – pour that repulsive foot slime into the vat and power up!"

"At once, my lord," purred the countess.

Sukka was already flicking switches beside the massive container. The platform hummed and creaked as it lowered the sinister, silent Toxitooth back into the minty sludge. As Blowdart pulled on a line of levers, Countess Kiss emptied the stinky yellow slime into the vat . . .

And suddenly, blinding white sparks of power crackled around it! The minty sludge inside bubbled like lava and foamed like an angry sea. A long, wiggly white arm banged and battered at the side of the tank. An enormous foot on the end of a long rope-like leg stuck up wildly into the air. Splashes and splats of sticky goo flew from the vat and then an awful creaking, scraping noise started up – the sound of giant teeth grinding together . . .

"He lives!" screamed Countess Kiss, as the lights flashed brighter and faster and the platform began to rise.

Plog stared at Furp in alarm. "I thought you said my slime would overload the chemicals?"

"It will!" Furp closed his eyes, shrinking into his pants like a tortoise into its shell. "Five, four, three, two, one . . ."

KER-BOOOOOOOOOM ! ! !

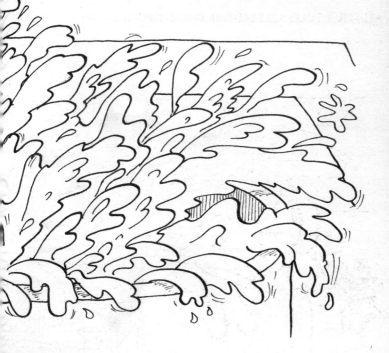

The vat went SPLAT! The explosion ripped through the lab! The force of it threw Plog off the couch and almost stripped the fur from his body. It blew Blowdart into Sukka, and both went crashing into the countess. Sludgy, slimy, minty sploshes rained down all around as controls sparked and smoked and light bulbs shattered. The mouth museum above was set shaking like a jelly in a hurricane; half the ceiling fell in and Furp was nearly flattened by falling debris.

"Nooooooooo!" Lord Klukk wailed from the smellyvision set. "Frog-face, you have buk-buk-betrayed me. You've destroyed my Toxitooth!"

"No, wait!" cried Countess Kiss. "Look, my lord – *Toxitooth still lives*!"

Furp peered out fearfully from under his crash helmet. "He does?"

"Uh-oh," said Plog, struggling against the sticky floss that bound him. "Looks like Big-mouth there was stronger than you thought, Furp!"

It was true. Standing in the middle of the ruined lab, his evil enamel agleam, was the terrifying Toxitooth. Opening his giant jaws, he let out a bloodcurdling, bone-rattling roar.

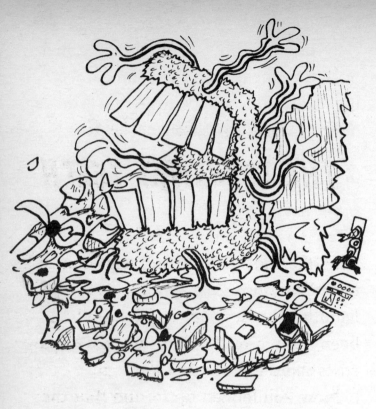

"Welcome to the world of the living, my pet," snarled Lord Klukk from the screen. "Let your first act be to deal with these slimy fools who tried to destroy you. EAT them, Toxitooth. DEVOUR THEM!"

Chapter Nine
THE TEARAWAY TEETH

The aftershocks of the lab explosion still rumbled and rocked through Curio's Mouth Museum. Zill and Danjo had been thrown to the floor as glass display cases shattered all around them.

Now Zill looked up to find that the big vault door had buckled in the blast.

"Danjo, quick," she breathed. "Maybe now you can smash it down?"

"Worth a try," Danjo agreed. With a yell, he ran and shoulder-charged the door.

It burst open with a CLANG! and then he and Zill leaped outside.

"All right, Curio," Danjo yelled, looking all around, braced for battle. "Take us to our friends — or else!"

But Curio hardly seemed to hear him, sitting on the floor in a quivering heap. "Look," he squeaked, gazing about at caved-in corridors and exploded exhibits. "My museum . . . it's ruined!"

Zill coughed on wisps of evil-smelling smoke. "Whatever caused this damage must have come from down in the basement — and that's where you said the countess had her secret lab."

"You're right," Curio realized. "Well, if she *is* responsible for that big bang I shall give her a jolly good speaking-to!"

"So will I," Danjo promised, raising his pincers. "Only, I'll let *these* do the talking!"

Zill and Danjo chased after Curio as he tore down the cracked and crumbling steps to the basement. A huge hole had been blown in the floor to reveal the secret lab underneath.

"Look!" Zill cried, pointing to the gigantic, drooling jaws-on-legs down below. "That must be Countess Kiss's home-made tooth-creature!"

"Oh, my!" Curio clutched his hands together dreamily. "It's *beautiful*!"

"*Poo*-tiful, more like," Danjo retorted. "And Plog and Furp are trapped in its path!" He aimed through the hole and squirted icy slime in front of the dental demon, building it up into a freezing blue barrier that blocked its advance.

"Danjo?" Plog looked up in amazement. "And Zill! You're here – and you've stopped Toxitooth!"

Zill and Danjo cheered – but the next moment, the toothy titan smashed through the slime-ice and continued its advance.

"Stopped it for two-point-seven seconds, anyway," said Furp ruefully.

"Plog, Furp – it's time for plan B," Zill yelled. "Slime-line coming down!" With a cough and a gurgle, she flicked out a thick slimy rope through the hole in the basement floor to the lab below. Although Plog's legs were still tied up, he had worked his arms free and now grabbed for the slime-line, as did Furp. Danjo helped Zill pull up on the sticky strand, and together they lifted their friends into the air. Enraged, Toxitooth tried to swat them with his long, skinny arms – but just missed.

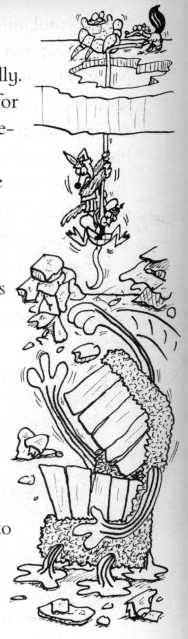

"Stop them, my Gobs," Countess Kiss shouted at Sukka and Blowdart. "Scrunch them! Squish them! Don't let Lord Klukk's chosen victims get away!"

"Hear that, Curio?" gasped Zill, still straining to lift Plog and Furp. "There's your 'sweet angel'!"

Curio looked shocked. "But, Countess," he cried, "I thought you were so gentle and kind!"

"That's because you are a nit-witty numbskull with the brains of a squashed baked bean!" sneered the countess. "You're no use to us any more, Curio – and once the Slime Squad is dealt with, YOU will be next!"

Curio squealed – and this time, his panic was for real. "Oh, no! Oh, mercy!" He collapsed to the floor. "Oh, help . . ."

"It's OK, Mr Curio," Plog shouted up to him, still dangling in midair. "Let fear disappear – the Slime Squad is here!"

Zill was so shocked she almost let go of the slime-line. "You did it!" she marvelled. "Plog, you finally got our battle cry right!"

"I did?" Plog beamed. "Hey, I did, didn't I!"

"Shame Curio's fainted," Danjo noted. "But I bet that if he'd heard you, he'd have been very comforted."

"There'll be no comfort for any of you," snarled Sukka, bouncing up onto the remains of the vat, his mouth opening wide. "Last time we met I was only playing around. Now – prepare to perish!"

The Gruesome Gob drew in an incredibly enormous breath. Plog and Furp clung on to Zill's slime-line for dear life as they found themselves pulled towards Sukka's gaping gob like dust into a horrible hoover. And as they dangled helplessly in midair, Toxitooth was lurching closer with every passing second . . .

"You're not as good as you think you are, Sukka," Plog gasped, pointing his legs at Sukka and wiggling his feet. "In fact, you should be given the boot. *Two* of them, to be precise!"

The Gruesome Gob realized too late that he was sucking the cast-iron, water-filled shoes from Plog's feet! CLUNK! BONG! Sukka wound up with two cast-iron kicks to his murderous mouth.

The impacts knocked him backwards into Blowdart, and both of them fell with a couple of splats into the ruins of the vat.

"Ha!" cried Plog. "As a sucker, Sukka – you suck!" Zill and Danjo quickly finished hauling him and Furp up out of the ruins of the lab, and Plog hugged them both. "Thank you!"

"Yes, thank you, my friends," Furp agreed. "But we're not out of the woods yet."

"Toxitooth!" Lord Klukk's desperate squawk rang out from the smellyvision screen in the lab. "Destroy the Slime Squad at once."

But Toxitooth took no notice, snarling and roaring.

"That is an order!" Kluck bellowed.

But again, he was ignored as the toothy fiend plodded on towards the far wall of the laboratory.

"Bad tooth-monster!" Countess Kiss yelled, running up behind Toxitooth. "Listen to your master – OOOF!" The filling-filled fury swiped her aside with a giant white hand and she went flying after her Gruesome Gobs into the squelchy shattered vat.

Plog winced. "She'll have a fat lip after a slap like that."

"It was fat enough already!" said Zill.

"But how come old Big-Tooth down there isn't following orders?" Danjo wondered.

"Er . . . that might be my fault," Furp admitted. "I added a super-strong dose of Plog's foot-slime to Klukk's life-making mixture, and it looks like it's made Toxitooth's tiny brain cells too toxic to take instructions from anyone."

"Nice work, Furp." Plog slapped him on the back. "Thanks to you, Lord Klukk doesn't have a mad, massive mouth-monster under his control."

"Instead, it's out of anyone's control!" Zill realized.

CHOMP! CRRUNNCH! The toothy terror began to chew and claw his way through the wall of the underground lab, eagerly swallowing down the mud and rubbish with gruff slurps and gurgles.

"Uh-oh." Danjo gulped as the floor began to shake. "If that toothy troublemaker smashes his way out, he could bring this whole place crashing down around us."

Furp nodded. "And he'll be free to rampage through Trashland. There's no telling what chaos he'll cause."

"Klukk!" Plog bellowed down at the smellyvision set as the museum shook harder. "You've seen your pet monster, he's running wild. How can we stop him?"

"You can't!" Lord Klukk cackled loudly. "He is like me – un-buk-buk-beatable. He will go on destroying until there is nothing left – including the four of you!"

"Is that what you want?" Plog jeered. "To be the ruler of an empty wilderness?"

"I shall buk-buk-build a NEW Trashland and fill it with more monsters of my own making," Klukk gloated. "I shall rule supreme."

Countess Kiss struggled out of the smashed-up vat of goo, her huge lips more swollen than ever. "But, my lord, please. What about me?"

"Who cares about you?" sneered Klukk. "You have failed me – so you can *kiss* your dreams of power buk-buk-bye-bye!" The shadowy image on the screen began to fade. "Farewell, fools . . ."

Toxitooth roared again and started punching and chewing his way out of the lab. The basement floor shook harder. More of the ruined lab ceiling crashed down on top of the vat, burying Countess Kiss and her Gruesome Gobs. Danjo had to grab hold of Zill to stop her slipping through the hole in the basement floor, as Toxitooth kept crunching his way to freedom.

"It's no good," Zill yelled. "That thing's going to chomp its way through our whole world – and there's nothing we can do to stop it!"

Chapter Ten

DENTAL DESTRUCTION!

As Toxitooth noshed and guzzled his
way out of the underground lair, Plog
bunched his fists. "We're not beaten
yet," he growled. "Come on, he'll
be tunnelling outside – let's head
him off!"

Carrying Curio between
them, Danjo and Furp
followed Zill and Plog up
the crumbling stairs
and into the
ruined hallway
of the main
museum.

Plog kicked open
the front door,
and the five of
them hurried
outside into
the overgrown
grounds.

"If only
we had some
water," panted
Zill.

Plog frowned. "You mean, we could
squirt some down Toxitooth's throat so
he's too busy drinking to eat?"

"Er, maybe." Zill was holding her
nose. "I actually meant that you could
use the water for your feet – now you've
lost your boots they're leaking that
stinky slime again!"

"Oops!" Plog looked down at his
gloopy feet and sighed. "Sorry, everyone.
Out of water, I just can't
help it."

Curio was coughing and croaking feebly in Danjo's arms. "Sounds like our friend here could use a little water himself."

"We don't have any water," said Furp. "But I'll bet a drop of my Slime-ade will do the trick." He pulled yet another bottle from his metal pants and sloshed some of the fizzy brew down Curio's throat.

"UGH!" Curio sat bolt upright, spluttering. "What IS that stuff?"

"Just my own special recipe," said Furp modestly. "Half-chewed boiled sweets, foot slime, fizzy water . . ."

"It's SO sugary. It should be illegal!" Curio cried. "A couple of bottles of that and all your teeth would fall out . . ."

"What?" Plog rounded on him sharply. "Seriously?"

"Absolutely!" Curio wiped his mouth. "And I should know – I run a mouth museum. I'm an expert on teeth."

"Of course you are. And if Slime-ade is really that bad for gnashers . . ." Plog pointed up to the large tub of Slime-ade on top of the Slime-mobile's invisible roof and looked at Zill, Furp and Danjo. "Guys, what if we could make Toxitooth drink that stuff? It might weaken his gnashers enough to slow him down, at least."

"It's worth a try," Zill agreed, and Danjo nodded.

Furp beamed proudly. "I knew carrying a good supply of Slime-ade around with us was a good idea!"

But suddenly, the earth shook and the huge, jagged outline of Toxitooth came clawing its way out of the ground, mud, earthworms and foil tops falling from its menacing molars. Zill's tail stiffened with fear as the creature gave a ravenous, mint-scented roar and lumbered away.

"He's heading into town," groaned Danjo. "If he starts chewing through the nearby neighbourhoods, hundreds of monsters could be hurt or killed."

"We've got to keep him here and get a gobful of Slime-ade down his throat," said Plog. "But how?"

Even as Plog asked the question, Toxitooth's terrifying jaws twitched, like he were somehow smelling the air.

119

Suddenly, the
giant jaws
swung round
and looked
down at
Plog,
hissing
hungrily.

"Fur-boy!"
Zill gasped.
"Toxitooth's
after YOU!"

"Oh dear," said Furp. "Our toothy
friend came to life after slurping your
foot slime – I suspect he's got a taste for
it!"

The gigantic mouth-monster lashed
out with a long twisty arm and grabbed
Plog around the chest. He lifted him
high into the air and shook him, like a
human might shake an all-but-empty
can into his mouth to catch the very last
drops.

120

"Plog!" Danjo yelled. "Don't let it eat you!"

"The thought had occurred to me!" Plog panted. His feet were dripping luminous sludge into Toxitooth's wide-open mouth – but just below him was the invisible roof of the Slime-mobile. With a desperate twist, Plog tore himself free of the creature's grip and landed with a thump beside the cauldron of sparkling Slime-ade. As Toxitooth gave a grating roar and lurched closer, Plog struggled to untie the ropes holding the cauldron in place. "Guys, help me!" he shouted.

Furp, Zill and Danjo were already clambering up to assist him, snapping through the ropes, sliding their fingers beneath the bottom of the cooking pot. Even Mr Curio joined them, the muscles in his four arms straining as he helped the Slime Squad tip the tub up, higher, higher, *higher* . . .

Then finally, as Toxitooth opened his giant jaws ready to devour them all, the cauldron overturned and an almighty torrent of super-sticky Slime-ade sloshed down the creature's formidable throat! And though he spluttered and gurgled, Toxitooth's gigantic jaws remained open, draining every last drop of the ultra-sugary liquid.

Furp smiled at Plog. "I used a little of your foot-slime to flavour this drink, remember? No wonder he loves it."

"But you know how it is," said Zill, watching bright-eyed as Toxitooth suddenly staggered backwards. "If you have too much sweet stuff, it will always make you sick . . ."

"Look!" squeaked Curio. The dental demon's humungous teeth were turning yellow. Tiny cracks were appearing in the enamel. A rotten bouquet of decay wafted from the creature's throat. Toxitooth choked and growled and started jumping on the spot, snapping his teeth in Plog's direction as if sensing he'd been tricked and wanting a nasty chewy revenge.

BOOOM! Klukk's creation struck the Slime-mobile with both fists; as it rocked, Plog lost his balance and tumbled heavily to the ground. The terrible Toxitooth loomed over him . . .

And then a new and different roar started up. The roar of a vehicle. To be precise, the roar of a white pick-up truck – zooming closer and closer at a very high speed.

"Look out, Plog!" Zill yelled. She spat out a slime-line. Plog grabbed for it and was yanked away just in time, as the pick-up rammed into the back of Toxitooth – and he burst into billions of pieces! Little toothy lumps rained down all around like pieces of grit. Then, with a screech of brakes, the white pick-up truck veered away, and Plog could see a bruised and battered Countess Kiss at the wheel with both her Gruesome Gobs lying dazed in the back.

"You killed Toxitooth!" cried Plog. "How come?"

"No one, but NO ONE, clobbers Countess Kiss and gets away with it!" she shouted back, pouting. "And since Lord Klukk was so rude to me, he deserves his plans to go to pieces!" She blew Plog a nasty, squelchy smooch. "So long, Ploggy-woggy. You know, if you weren't such a goody two-shoes, you'd be quite cute. Byeeeeeeeee!"

"Ploggy-woggy?" Plog grimaced as the pick-up roared away. "Less of your lip!" he yelled after her.

Zill laughed. "The countess has gone, the gobs have gone, Toxitooth's gone – the danger's gone!"

"For now," said Furp with a worried look. "We don't know where Lord Klukk is, but I'll bet he's already working on another way to take over Trashland."

"If he is," said Danjo, "we'll be ready for him."

"And if you need any extra help," said Curio, grinning away, "please, call on me. I feel so bad about helping Countess Kiss to capture you."

"You helped us in the end," Plog reminded him.

"But, er . . . how come you're so happy?" asked Zill. "Your museum's been trashed, half your exhibits are broken and you've got the biggest hole in your basement ever – but you look over the moon. Why?"

"Why? WHY?" Curio grabbed her front paws and twirled her round in a little dance of happiness. "Just look at all these tiny bits of teeth that Toxitooth's turned into. Once I've found them all and glued them all together, I'll have the most amazing display for my mouth museum EVER!" He picked up two tiny nuggets and held them to his chest. "Just imagine . . . It'll be a fly-away hit! A roaring success! It won't take me long — I reckon I could be ready to open again in as little as seven years!"

Plog smiled. "In the meantime, perhaps you could make some false teeth for the rats, foxes and field-mice who had theirs stolen by the countess and her gobs?"

"Good thinking," said Curio. "I can use the drill made for the Purple Ponkwasher – if the animals hold still long enough . . ."

"Yes, well. Good luck with that." Plog shook his head as the crazy curator wandered away, back into his museum. "Don't forget to invite us to the grand re-opening!"

"I'm washing my fur that day," said Zill flatly. She yawned. "Wow, I'm tired. What time is it?"

Furp checked the alarm clock in his pants. "Two-thirty in the morning."

"You mean, *tooth-hurty!*" joked Danjo.

"If you're making jokes like that then it's definitely time for a nap," Plog declared. "And when bedtime looms large . . ."

"The Slime Squad shout CHARRRRRGE!" cried Furp, Zill and Danjo.

The four friends leaped into the Slime-mobile and Zill drove them home to catch some zeds and charge up their batteries – ready for their next super-slimy adventure.

The Squaddies will return in
THE SLIME SQUAD
vs
THE CYBER-POOS

HAVE YOU READ
THE SLIME SQUAD'S FIRST
AMAZING ADVENTURE?

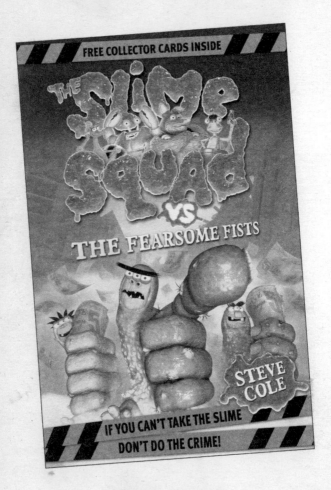

Out now!